A MAGIC CIRCLE BOOK

Monkey's Tail

Rabbit's Cup

retold by **LOIS M. TURNER**
illustrated by **FRANK BOZZO**

THEODORE CLYMER
SENIOR AUTHOR, READING 360

GINN AND COMPANY
A XEROX COMPANY

Library of Congress Catalog Card Number: 76–162051

International Standard Book Number: 0–663–22975–8

Monkey's Tail

One day while Wolf was walking
through the woods and thinking of food,
he stepped into a deep hole. He tried to
jump out many times, but he only fell
down deeper. Wolf stayed in the hole
for three days without food or water.
At last he thought that if he howled as
loudly as he could, help would come.
He howled and he howled.

Sometime later when Monkey came by, he heard Wolf's howl and walked over to the hole. "Who's making all that noise?" Monkey asked.

"It's your friend Wolf. I fell in this hole and I can't get out. You must help me."

Monkey looked down at Wolf. Wolf looked back at Monkey with his big, unhappy eyes.

"But how can I help you?" asked Monkey. "I'm so small and you're so big. Why don't you jump out?"

"I can't," said Wolf. "I just fall down deeper and deeper."

"Well, what do you want me to do?" asked Monkey.

Wolf could see that there was a tree right beside the hole. "Catch on to that tree," he said to Monkey, "and let your tail fall into the hole so I can hold on and get out."

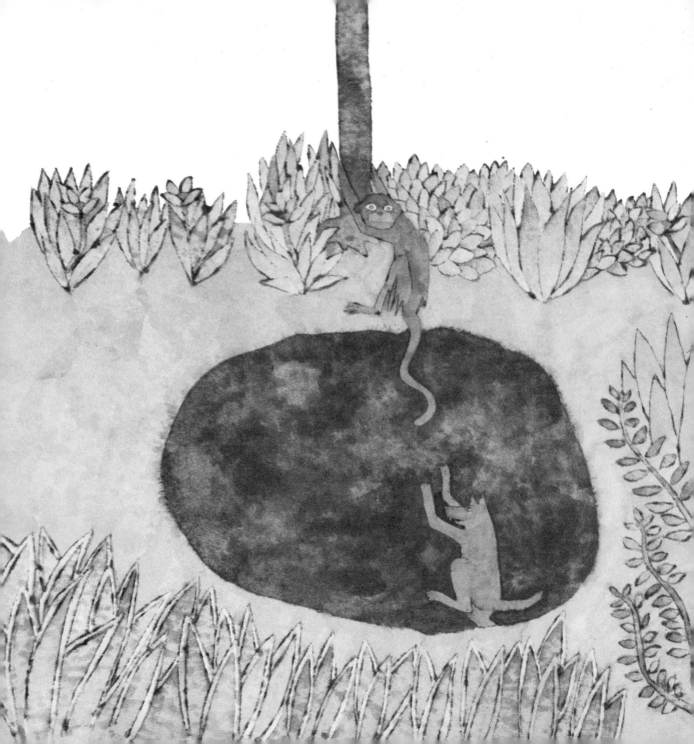

Monkey did as Wolf asked and soon Wolf was out of the hole. But Wolf still held Monkey's tail.

"I have had no food for days," Wolf said. "I don't like to do this, but I must eat you."

Monkey begged Wolf not to eat him. "Please, Wolf. I helped you. You can't eat me. I'm your friend."

But Monkey soon saw that all his talking would not make Wolf let him go. At last Monkey said, "If you want to be fair, you will let me go and then try to catch me. Then if you catch me, you will have the right to eat me." Still Wolf would not let go.

As they talked, Tortoise came by. "What's all the talk about?" he asked.

Monkey said, "Wolf was down in that hole, and as I came by I heard him calling for help. I helped him and now he wants to eat me!"

"Is this so?" asked Tortoise.

Wolf would not look Tortoise in the
eye. Still holding Monkey's tail he said,
"Yes, it is so."

Now, all the animals thought Tortoise was wise. So Monkey asked Tortoise, "What do you say Wolf must do?"

Tortoise wanted to keep Wolf for a friend, but even more he wanted to help Monkey. Tortoise thought fast and said, "Before I can tell you what to do, the two of you must clap your hands three times."

He told Monkey to clap first. Then
it was Wolf's turn. When Wolf let go
of Monkey's tail to clap his hands,
Tortoise called, "Run, Monkey! Run for
your life!"

Monkey ran to the top of a tall tree.
Tortoise went into some tall grass to
hide, and Wolf was left alone.

Rabbit's Cup

There once was a rabbit king who
had a beautiful daughter. Many animals
who lived in the town wanted to marry
her, but she didn't like any of them.
Her father thought she was too hard to
please.

One day he said, "I will ask
many to come from far away to do a
very hard thing. The one who drinks a
cup of hot, hot water without stopping
once may marry my daughter."

When the news was sent out, many
animals came at once to see the king.
Lion, Bear, Eagle, Wolf, Fox, Monkey,
and Mouse each tried to drink the hot
water. One by one they said the water
was too hot.

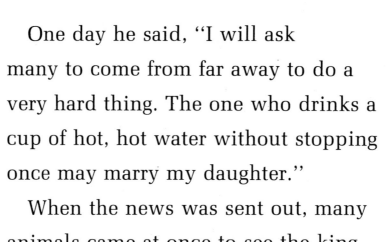

Now, a rabbit who lived far away in
the big woods heard the news. He, too,
wanted a chance to win the king's
daughter. The rabbit had many brothers
and sisters and he asked them to go
with him to see the king.

Behind Rabbit's back his brothers and sisters shook their heads and said to one another, "Drink hot water! How can it be? Everyone knows our brother is scared of everything hot! He can't win the hand of the king's daughter." But they went along lippety, lippety, just to see what would happen.

At the king's house, Rabbit went
before the king, bowed low, and said,
"I have come to win your beautiful
daughter for my wife." Lion, Bear,
Eagle, Wolf and all the other animals
laughed. But Rabbit turned to the king
and asked for the hot water.

When the king gave him the cup,
Rabbit said, "Good King, my brothers
and sisters here don't think this water
is hot. May I let them see how hot the
cup is before I begin to drink?"

The rabbit king thought, "Why not?"
He didn't want Rabbit's brothers and
sisters to think that what he said was
not true. So he let Rabbit hand the cup
to each of his many brothers and sisters.

The cup went from hand to hand, and each rabbit saw that the water was just as hot as the king had said. It was far too hot to drink. But by the time all the brothers and sisters had touched the cup and had handed it back to Rabbit, the water was no longer hot. Rabbit could drink it without stopping once.

That is how Rabbit won the king's beautiful daughter for his wife.

ABCDEFGHIJK 7654321
PRINTED IN THE UNITED STATES OF AMERICA